THE
CHICKENHOUSE
HOUSE

Books by Ellen Howard

Circle of Giving

When Daylight Comes

Gillyflower

Edith Herself

Her Own Song

Sister

The Chickenhouse House

The Chickenhouse House

by Ellen Howard
illustrated by Nancy Oleksa

A JEAN KARL BOOK
Atheneum   1991   New York

Collier Macmillan Canada
Toronto
Maxwell Macmillan International Publishing Group
New York   Oxford   Singapore   Sydney

Atheneum
Macmillan Publishing Company
866 Third Avenue
New York, NY 10022

Collier Macmillan Canada, Inc.
1200 Eglinton Avenue East
Suite 200
Don Mills, Ontario M3C 3N1

First Edition
Printed in the United States of America
10 9 8 7 6 5 4 3 2 1

Library of Congress Cataloging-in-Publication Data

Howard, Ellen.
The chickenhouse house / Ellen Howard. — 1st ed.
p.   cm.
"A Jean Karl book."
Summary: When Alena and her family move onto new farmland out
on the prairie, they must live at first in the chickenhouse because
there is no time to build a house before winter; then with the warm
weather comes the excitement of watching the big new house go up.
ISBN 0-689-31695-X
[1. Frontier and pioneer life—Fiction.   2. Dwellings—Fiction.]
I. Title.
PZ7.H83274Ch   1991

[E]—dc20   90-38007

For Kristin and Joel,
who got used to *their* new houses
—E. H.

Father "hauled lumber over a trail &
through the Prairie
grass . . . to build a large chicken house
with several
windows and lined throughout which was
lived in while
the 6 roomed house was being constructed,
with a large
full sized cellar and beautiful winding
stairway made of black walnut wood."
— from my great-aunt Ruth's "memory
book," written in 1970 when she was 90
years old

CONTENTS

❧ 1 ❧

Moving

For almost an hour, the wagon had bumped along the trail through grass as high as the horses' backs. Alena sat between Mother and Father on the wagon seat, holding Father's gold watch. Her little brother William rode on a pile of quilts behind the seat. Baby Fritz snuggled in Mother's arms. The bed of the wagon was loaded with furniture and boxes and baskets of household goods.

Father pulled back on the reins, and the wagon stopped at the crest of a rise. The horses dropped down their heads and blew great, whuffling breaths into the chill autumn air.

"Here we are," Father said.

Alena looked at the round face of Father's watch.

"An hour," she said. "It took an hour, just as you said."

Father traced an arc in the air with his hand.

"It's all ours as far as the eye can see," he said. "Good, rich land of our own."

Mother shaded her eyes against the sun and looked. Then she nodded and smiled.

"At last," she said.

Alena shaded her eyes as Mother had done. She looked out over the gold prairie grass. Not a bush or a shrub could she see on the land, not a house or a barn or a shed. Only, some distance away, a few cottonwood trees grew along a creek.

"Where is it?" Alena said.

"Where is what?" said Father.

"Where is the farm Grandfather has given us?"

Father laughed his low, chuckling laugh.

"This is it, little 'Lena," he said.

"But where is the house? Where is the barn?" said Alena.

Father said, "We will build them by and by. For now, there is only the chicken-house."

Father clucked to the horses, and the wagon rolled down the slope toward the cottonwood trees. They splashed across the creek where the bank was low and drove into a meadow on the other side.

In the meadow stood a small frame

building, one story high, with a stout wooden door and five narrow glass windows.

"The chickenhouse," Father said.

"It will do nicely," said Mother.

"Why do the chickens want windows?" Alena said.

Father laughed again.

"Why, I don't reckon the chickens care, little 'Lena," he said. "*We* want windows in *this* chickenhouse."

"Oh, Alena," Mother said. "You haven't been listening. We told you we haven't time before winter sets in to build a house. Father and Grandfather and Uncle Clark have built our chickenhouse first. We'll live in it for now."

Father gently took his watch from Alena's hand. He lifted her off the wagon seat and set her on the ground. Alena hung her

4

winter with my folks," he said to Mother. "The chickenhouse won't be as comfortable for you and the children as the homeplace is."

"*This* is *our* homeplace," said Mother.

William fell out of the window onto his head and set up a fearful howl.

Mother hurried to pick him up and brush him off.

Baby Fritz cried to keep him company.

"We will have our table and our chairs and all our beds to make the chickenhouse homey," Father said, patting Alena's shoulder. He carried the chairs away to the chickenhouse.

Alena sat on the blanket beside the fussy baby. She looked at the chickenhouse. It did not look homey to her.

❧ 2 ❧

Settling

Alena was tired that night, but she could not go to sleep. She lay awake, listening to the wind sigh through the prairie grass. An owl hooted. Cricket frogs sang from the trees by the creek. These were not the night sounds Alena was used to. She was used to the cows lowing and the horses stamping in their stalls in Grandfather's barn. She was used to the grown-ups talking in Grandmother's downstairs sitting room.

She was used to the whisper of oak leaves on the upstairs windowpane.

The straw-tick of Mother's and Father's big bed rustled nearby. Alena heard a padding of bare feet on the floor. A dark shadow bent over her. She felt Mother's hands tuck the quilts more snugly around her. Mother's lips touched her forehead.

"Go to sleep now, Alena," Mother said.

In the morning, Alena opened her eyes when she heard the *chunk-chunk* of firewood being put into the stove. She scrambled to sit up, then pulled the warm quilt around her shoulders. Her breath made little clouds in the cold air.

Mother's head poked around the blanket that divided the chickenhouse into two rooms.

"Rise and shine, Alena," she said. "Grandfather and Uncle Clark will be here soon to help build a shed for the horses and Topsy."

Alena snuggled back into the warm nest of her quilt.

I *knew* it would be cold, she thought.

Father and Grandfather and Uncle Clark worked all day. They paced off the ground a distance behind the chickenhouse and pounded stakes into the dirt. They hammered and sawed. There was no time to sit on Grandfather's lap for a story. There was no time for Uncle Clark to make willow whistles for her and William.

"Fetch me that keg of nails, little 'Lena," Father called. "Hand me my hammer, please."

Alena ran to and fro, fetching, until her legs ached.

William slipped away to fish in the creek with a pin on a string, but he didn't catch any fish.

Baby Fritz crawled about on the trampled-down grass and ate bugs.

When Grandfather and Uncle Clark drove away that evening, a small shed barn had risen behind the chickenhouse. The next day, Father built stalls for the horses and Topsy.

Topsy seemed to like her funny little barn. She munched peacefully on the dry prairie grass in her new manger while Mother milked her that evening.

"So-o-o, Topsy," Mother crooned.

Alena leaned her forehead against Topsy's warm shoulder.

"Don't you miss your big barn, Topsy?" she whispered. "Don't you miss your calf and the other cows and Grandfather's oxen and horses?"

But Topsy just chewed.

Alena listened to the sound of her chew-

12

ing and the deep, soft sound of her breath. She liked those sounds and the singing sound of Mother's voice and the ringing sound of the milk in the pail. Still, she wished she and Mother and Topsy were in Grandfather's barn with its long row of stalls and its high haymow.

In the soft, Indian summer days that followed, Father burned off prairie grass on a nearby rise. Clouds of smoke thickened the air. The jays circled, squawking, above the trees.

Alena helped Mother unpack the last of their things. Her eyes stung and she cried, perhaps because of the smoke.

William tried to stack fruit jars on a shelf, but he dropped one and broke it on the floor.

Baby Fritz fussed.

Grandmother has no one to help her now, Alena thought sadly, rubbing her eyes.

⚔ 3 ⚔
Fall

When the rain began, Alena pressed her nose to the windowpane and watched the rain walk on the grass, flattening it in waves.

When the sky cleared, Alena and William went out to play. The plovers and yellow-legs ran on the mud. Overhead, wild geese cried. Alena's skirts dragged through the wet grass and grew heavy. William ran, like the plovers, not slowed by skirts, but he fell down in the mud.

Mother cleaned up William and set him

to playing blocks while Alena changed her dress. They hung the wet things by the stove to dry. The fire in the stove glowed red.

Baby Fritz napped in his crib.

Alena sat at one end of the table and looked at a book.

At the other end of the table, Mother shaped bread loaves with floury hands.

The chickenhouse smelled of wet wool and wood smoke. Again the rain tapped on the roof.

"Will we live in the chickenhouse always?" said Alena.

"I have told you before, Alena," Mother said. "We will live in the chickenhouse until our new house is built."

Alena thought about that. It would take a long time to build a house, she thought. In the meantime, it was rather nice, listening to the rain on the roof of the chickenhouse house.

On Thanksgiving Day, Mother and Father and Alena and William and Baby Fritz drove in the wagon to Grandfather's house. The house was full of uncles and aunts and cousins in all sizes.

Grandmother hugged Alena hard.

"I miss my little helper," she said.

"I'm your helper now, aren't I, Grand-mother?" Cousin Emily said, pulling on Grandmother's arm.

"Yes, you are a good help," Grandmother said, and she hugged Emily, too.

Alena and William and the cousins ran up and down the stairs, playing hide-and-seek. Alena peeked into the room where she used to sleep, but her bed wasn't there anymore. Instead, a strange bed with a strange blue quilt stood by the window that looked out on the oak.

Mother and Father sat with the aunts and uncles at the long table in the dining

J 5256

room. Alena and William sat with the cousins at the round kitchen table. In the dining room, Grandfather said a long grace. In the kitchen, the cousins held hands and gave thanks quickly with Grandmother.

They all ate roast beef and chicken, potatoes and dressing and thick giblet gravy, cucumber pickles and tomato preserves, buns and butter and crab-apple jelly, and pumpkin pie with cream.

But after they finished, Alena's head hurt. Her stomach was too full, and so was the house—too full of people and voices and smells.

The aunts and uncles talked and talked.

William pulled Alena's hair.

Cousin Emily stuck out her tongue at her.

Alena was glad when Father said it was time to go home to the chickenhouse house.

✤ 4 ✤

Winter

When the sleet and snow came, Alena and William played checkers on the rug in front of the stove.

William licked the frosty windowpane and got his tongue stuck. Mother unstuck it with teakettle water.

Baby Fritz took his first steps, holding on to chairs and to Alena's hands.

At night, Alena could hear the wind howl across the prairie. But she could also hear

William breathe through his stuffed-up nose. She could hear Baby Fritz cry in his sleep. She could hear the fire crackle and Mother's soft laugh and the chuckle of Father's voice.

On Christmas Eve, a blizzard was blowing.

"If this doesn't let up," Father said, "we shan't be able to go to Grandfather's house for Christmas dinner."

"Will Saint Nicholas come in a blizzard?" William wanted to know.

"Will Saint Nicholas know there are *children* in this chickenhouse?" said Alena.

"Saint Nicholas isn't stopped by blizzards," said Mother, "and his *favorite* children live in a chickenhouse house."

When Alena opened her eyes on Christmas morning, she smelled cinnamon rolls. At the foot of her bed was her gray woolen stocking, lumpy and bumpy where it had been flat. She crawled out of her quilt, and William awoke.

"Saint Nicholas came! Looky what he brought!" cried William, running with his stocking to Mother and Father.

Alena held her stocking close to her chest. She climbed out of bed.

Mother and Father were drinking their coffee at the red-checked table.

William was shaking his stocking onto the rug—mittens, an orange, a clatter of walnuts, a green candy stick, a box of dominoes.

Alena climbed onto Father's lap, pulling her cold feet up under her nightdress. She held her stocking tight, feeling its lumps and bumps.

"Open your stocking," William cried.

But Alena couldn't just then. It was

enough to sit on Father's lap before the fire. She ate a hot cinnamon roll. She hugged her full stocking. She watched the snow swirl at the windows of the chickenhouse house. Alena wasn't a bit sorry they weren't going to Grandfather's.

🌿 5 🌿

Spring

The spells of heavy snow and soaking rain gave way at last to longer and longer spells of sunny days.

On Sundays, when the weather was dry, Father and Mother and Alena and William and Baby Fritz drove into town to church. On Easter, the children were given little cards with Bible verses on them.

Alena and William found violets and Johnny-jump-ups and little-boys'-breeches blooming near the creek.

Father got up before the sun to plow the fields he had cleared last fall.

"Will we live in the chickenhouse always?" Alena asked Mother.

Mother was churning butter. She pushed down the churn paddle and pulled it up with a jerk. Her answer came in little jerks, too, between the strokes of the paddle. "When Father . . . has gotten . . . the oats and . . . the corn in . . . he will start . . . building a . . . new house for . . . us."

"I have gotten used to the chickenhouse house," said Alena.

Mother stopped churning and pushed back her hair.

"Well, I haven't," she said. "I will be glad to have a big, new house."

Robins and thrushes sang in the cottonwoods.

Mother planted a garden—lettuce and radishes and little spring onions.

Alena fetched water from the creek.

Father broadcast the oats. Then he dragged the harrow back and forth across the field behind the team of horses to cover up the seed.

Baby Fritz had to be tied to the doorpost with a cotton rope to keep him from wandering.

One morning, after a night of heavy wind, Alena found a bird's nest blown from a tree. There were three little eggs in it, bright blue and unbroken.

She ran to the chickenhouse to fetch her Christmas mittens. Wearing them so her little-girl smell wouldn't get on the nest, she picked it up. She climbed as high as she dared into the tree. She set the nest in the crook of a branch.

"Here's your house back," she called to the birds.

But the mother bird did not return to

the nest. The next time the wind blew, the eggs were broken when the nest fell down.

"The mother bird is building a fine, new nest somewhere else," Mother told Alena.

But Alena thought it was sad that the bird had left her nice little nest.

🌿 6 🌿

Summer

When the corn had been planted, Father began to dig a hole. He dug it on the rise of ground he had burned off last fall. Every day, it grew deeper and wider. Some days, Grandfather and Uncle Clark came to help. Other days, a neighbor came with his grown-up sons. The hole had steep, up-and-down sides. Soon it was deeper than Father's head was high and as square and big as a room.

"It is our cellar," said Mother. "We will store our apples in it, and our pickles and preserves, our sauerkraut jar and our vinegar barrel."

"Where will we get the apples?" Alena said, looking out at the treeless prairie.

Mother smiled and put her arm around Alena's shoulders.

"Father will plant an orchard next year," she said. "Apples and peaches and cherries and plums. But until our trees bear, Grandfather will share his fruit with us."

Alena tried to imagine apple trees growing where now the grass stood high.

"I reckon I'll be grown by then," she said.

Alena loved to hang her head over the edge of the cellar hole and look down until she was dizzy.

Father was lining it with smooth stone slabs.

31

"To keep it cool in summertime," he said.

Then he built a stone foundation all around the cellar.

"For the house," he said.

"Is *this* the start of our big, new house?" said Alena.

"Why, of course it is, little 'Lena," he said. "Did you think we would live in the cellar?"

Alena had not thought they would live in the cellar. But she had gotten so used to the chickenhouse, she had almost forgotten the big, new house.

Alena helped Mother plant potato eyes and beans and squash and pumpkin seeds.

William tried to help, but he trampled on the rows. Mother sent him to play with Baby Fritz who was cross with teething.

Soon the only coolness was in the dewy morning. By eight o'clock, it was so hot the jays and the flickers stopped singing.

Then one day, Grandfather and Grandmother, the aunts and uncles and a whole lot of neighbors came to help build the house. Wagon after wagon drove into the shade of the cottonwood trees. The men climbed down with their tools in boxes, the women with baskets of food. The women left jars of tea and root beer in the creek to cool. They lugged the baskets to the chickenhouse.

Alena was glad to see her cousins and friends, glad it was house-raising day.

She played ball-and-base and pull-away with the other children. Between games, she helped fetch cool drinks for the thirsty working men.

Her cheeks grew hot. Dark spots danced before her eyes. But she could not keep still. She ran here and there, shrill with excitement.

33

Everywhere, everyone was busy and noisy, building the house.

When evening came, the frame of the house, two stories high, rose above new plank floors.

Alena and Cousin Emily walked around inside it, trying to see where the walls would go, and the windows and doors. It smelled of raw lumber. Alena thought it was spacious and grand.

Mother called them to supper, spread on cloths down by the creek. They went with dragging steps.

William fell asleep with his spoon in his hand. Father carried him to the chicken-house and put him to bed with Baby Fritz.

But Alena was allowed to sit up late to hear the grown-ups talk and sing. They rested beside the tents the men had pitched in the meadow. Alena watched fireflies flicker through the grass. She lay down on her back to look at the stars.

She woke when Father lifted her to carry her to bed. A light shone cozily from a window of the chickenhouse house to guide them through the dark.

By the time Grandfather and Grandmother, the aunts and the uncles, and the whole lot of neighbors went home the next afternoon, the new house was roofed and sided.

"Now will we live in our new house?" said Alena.

"As soon as the carpenter has finished the stairs," Mother said. "As soon as the cellar has been whitewashed, and the wallpaper has been hung, and the rugs are put down, and the stove is set up, and the rest of our furniture is brought from Grandfather's, and. . . ."

Alena stopped listening. She could see that it would be quite a long time yet before they moved out of the chickenhouse house.

cupboard in the dining room. The Bible was on the marble-topped table in the center of the parlor. The organ and the sofa and the whatnot marched along the wall-papered parlor walls.

Alena thought it all looked grand.

Upstairs, Mother was making the beds. Mother's and Father's big bed was in the front bedroom. Fritz's crib and William's bed were in the middle room. Alena's bed stood all alone in the room at the back.

Suddenly Alena had a funny feeling at the bottom of her stomach. Her room looked big and bare.

"This will be nice, having a room of your own," said Mother as she shook Alena's pillow into a pillowcase.

Alena went to the window. It was an upstairs window just like the one she had had at Grandfather's house. Kneeling beside it, she put her chin on her arm on the sill.

There was no oak tree outside this win
dow. Instead, Alena saw a small hump of
darkness lonely in the meadow by the
creek. It was the chickenhouse house.

"Into your nightdress," said Mother. "It's
time to go to sleep. I'll come tuck you in a
moment when I've got the boys to bed."

Slowly Alena folded her dress and pin-
afore, her petticoats and chemise. She put
them on her chair all by herself. She pulled
on her nightdress and climbed under the
quilt all by herself. Over her head, the ceil-
ing seemed far away, and shadows gath-
ered in its corners.

Alena was tired, but she could not go to
sleep. After Mother tucked her in, she lay
awake, listening for sounds in the big, new
house.

She could not hear William breathing or
Baby Fritz crying. She could not hear the
fire or Mother's laugh or Father's voice.

When she closed her eyes, she thought she could see the shadow of the chickenhouse house, lonely and silent in the meadow. There was a hard, hurting lump in her throat.

Alena climbed out of bed. She pulled her quilt around her shoulders and crept to the door. The landing was quiet and dark, but a faint glow of lamplight washed up the stairs.

One step at a time, Alena climbed down toward the light. Beneath her cold feet, the steps felt solid and icy smooth.

The light from the parlor spilled into the hall. Alena almost went toward it. Then Father said something, and Mother answered. In the strange, long hallway of the big, new house, their voices seemed different and far away.

Alena turned toward the kitchen. The fire in the stove burned low, but Alena

42

could feel its warmth. Without the stove, the chickenhouse would be cold.

She opened the door softly and went out into the night.

The moon showed her the way. The door of the chickenhouse house stood open, waiting for her.

Alena went in. The dirt floor was cold to her feet. There was no rug.

Alena could hear her own breathing, quick and loud. There was no table, no chairs or beds. The chickenhouse felt strange.

But now Alena was very tired. Her feet were cold. It seemed a long way to go back to the house. The moon was behind a cloud.

Alena curled up in her quilt in a corner. She pulled her feet inside her nightdress. She pulled the quilt around her ears. She was shaking with crying and cold.

Now there was no place she was used to, she thought. Not Grandfather's house where Cousin Emily now lived. Not the big, new house, grand though it was. Not even the chickenhouse house!

Alena woke to lantern light hurting in her eyes.

"What are you doing out here, little 'Lena?" Father was saying, worry in his voice.

Alena did not know what to answer, but she was glad Father had come to find her.

"Little 'Lena, little 'Lena," Father said, picking her up. "We live in the big house now. We don't live in the chickenhouse."

Alena put her arms around Father's neck. She rested her head on his shoulder as he carried her back. The cool air touched her eyelids as she rode in his arms through the night. His whiskers brushed her cheek.

45

❧ 8 ❧

The Chickenhouse

Alena woke to silence the next morning. She lay in the tangle of her quilt and listened. Then she heard Baby Fritz's cry and William's feet on the stairs.

"Time to get up, Mother says," William cried.

Alena sat up and swung her legs over the side of the bed. Her breath made little clouds in the air. The wooden floor was icy. She grabbed her clothes and raced after William, who was running back down-stairs.

Mother was at the kitchen range, frying bacon.

Baby Fritz was tied in a chair.

The kitchen was warm and steamy. It smelled of stove blacking and bacon and paint.

When Alena came outside after helping with the breakfast dishes, she saw William down by the creek. She could hear Father hammering over by Topsy's shed. She wandered over to watch.

"Hand me a nail, little 'Lena," Father said. "Hold this board, please."

Alena helped until Father had to go see to the horses. Then she walked down to the creek, but William was nowhere to be found.

Finally, kicking at clumps of yellow grass,

Alena went once again to the chickenhouse.

The stout wooden door hung open. The five narrow windows looked dirty and small.

Alena walked all around the chickenhouse. She looked in the windows. She went inside.

The chickenhouse was dim and bare. It smelled of dirt. Pale sunlight filtered through the stovepipe hole.

Alena closed her eyes. She imagined the way the fire used to glow in the stove. She imagined how cozy it was to lie in bed and listen to the voices on the other side of the blanket. She imagined the way the chickenhouse had smelled when Mother baked bread.

Alena heard footsteps. Father pushed through the doorway, carrying the nesting boxes he had been building.

"Why, hello, little 'Lena," he said. "Want to help me put these in? We have to hurry because Grandfather is bringing us two dozen chicks tomorrow."

Alena handed nails to Father, one at a time, from the little nail keg.

"Don't you like our big, new house, little 'Lena?" Father said after a while.

Alena put her head to one side and thought.

"I thought I would like it," she said. "But it is too big."

"We wanted it big so there would be room for us to grow," said Father.

"It is a long way from my bedroom to yours," said Alena. "It is a long way downstairs, too. I can't hear us as I could in the chickenhouse house."

"That is true," said Father, hammering in a nail.

"It is cold in the morning," said Alena.

50

"I thought you used to say the chicken-house was cold," said Father.

"Did I say that?" Alena tried to remember.

"I believe you did," said Father.

"Well, I got used to the chickenhouse house," Alena said. "I got to liking it."

"Do you think you might get used to our big, new house in time?" said Father, lifting up another nesting box.

Alena looked around the chickenhouse. With the nesting boxes in place, it was looking more like a house for chickens. She thought about two dozen fluffy yellow chicks coming to live in it. She thought of their peeping. She thought of the way they would scratch at the smooth dirt floor. She thought about throwing them handfuls of corn and watching them peck it up.

"Will the chicks like our chickenhouse?" she said.

"What do *you* think?" said Father.

"It is the right size for chickens," Alena said thoughtfully. "The windows let in the light. If we fill the nests with straw and cover up the stovepipe hole, the chicks will keep warm."

"Yes," said Father.

"But I think," Alena said, "it *may* take a little while for the chicks to get used to their chickenhouse house."